HERE'S THE STORY, IN A NUTSHELL:

I NEVER leave my nut tree.
It's way too dangerous out there.
I could encounter germs, poison ivy
or sharks.

If danger comes along, I'm prepared.
I have antibacterial soap, Band-Aids
and a parachute.

But things really get shaken up later
in the book when I'm forced out of
my tree by a vicious intruder!

Will I survive this ordeal?
Will I undergo a life-changing
experience?
Will I discover my true inner self?

**READ MY NUTTY ADVENTURE TO
FIND OUT ...**

✱ Caution: This story is not suitable
for green Martians.

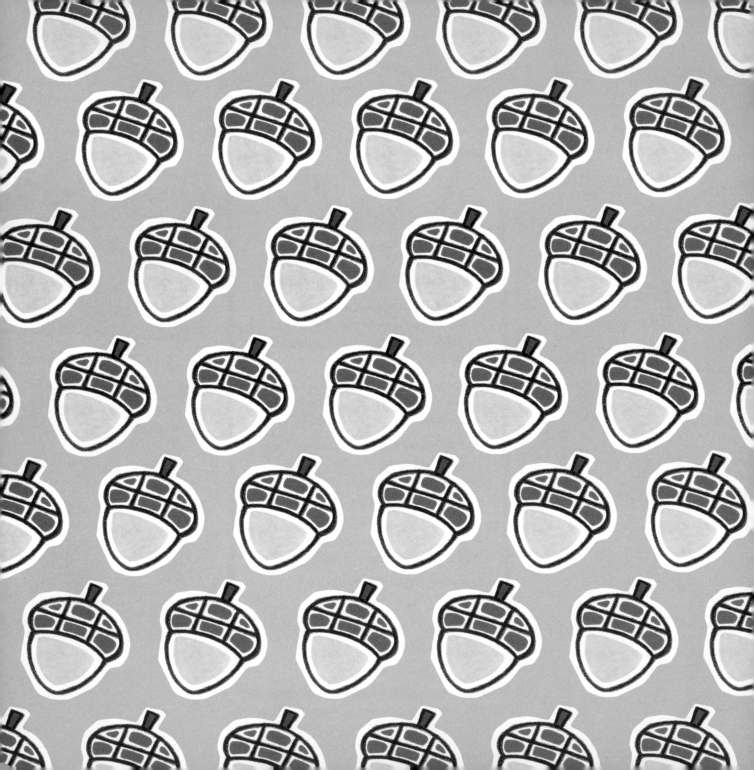

WARNING!

Scaredy Squirrel insists that everyone wash their hands with antibacterial soap before reading this book.

For Francine and Hubert

First paperback edition 2008

Text and illustrations © 2006 Mélanie Watt

This edition is only available for distribution through the school market by Scholastic Book Fairs and Scholastic Canada, Ltd.

ISBN 978-1-55453-404-3 (pbk.)

CM PA 08 0 9 8 7 6 5 4 3 2

Kids Can Press acknowledges the financial support of the Government of Ontario, through the Ontario Media Development Corporation's Ontario Book Initiative; the Ontario Arts Council; the Canada Council for the Arts; and the Government of Canada, through the BPIDP, for our publishing activity.

Published in Canada by
Kids Can Press Ltd.
29 Birch Avenue
Toronto, ON M4V 1E2

Published in the U.S. by
Kids Can Press Ltd.
2250 Military Road
Tonawanda, NY 14150

www.kidscanpress.com

The artwork in this book was rendered in charcoal pencil and acrylic.
The text is set in Potato Cut.

Edited by Tara Walker
Designed by Mélanie Watt and Karen Powers
Printed and bound in China

The hardcover edition of this book is smyth sewn casebound.
The paperback edition of this book is limp sewn with a drawn-on cover.

CM 06 0 9 8 7 6
CM PA 08 0 9 8 7 6 5 4 3 2 1

LIBRARY AND ARCHIVES CANADA CATALOGUING IN PUBLICATION

Watt, Mélanie, 1975-
Scaredy squirrel / by Mélanie Watt.
ISBN 978-1-55337-959-1 (bound). ISBN 978-1-55453-023-6 (pbk.)
I.Title.
PS8645.A884S28 2006   jC813'.6   C2005-903572-2

Kids Can Press is a ℓℴℛℯ𝒰𝒮™ Entertainment company

Scaredy Squirrel

by Mélanie Watt

KIDS CAN PRESS

Scaredy Squirrel never leaves his nut tree.

He'd rather stay in his safe and familiar tree than risk venturing out into the unknown. The unknown can be a scary place for a squirrel.

A few things
Scaredy Squirrel
is afraid of:

tarantulas

poison ivy

green Martians

killer bees

germs

sharks

So he's perfectly happy
to stay right where he is.

Advantages of never leaving the nut tree:

- great view

- plenty of nuts

- safe place

- no 🦀 🍁 👾 🐝 🐝 ⚜ 🌊

Disadvantages of never leaving the nut tree:

- same old view

- same old nuts

- same old place

Monday

Tuesday

Wednesday

Thursday   Friday   Saturday   Sunday

In Scaredy Squirrel's nut tree, every day
is the same. Everything is predictable.
All is under control.

Scaredy Squirrel's daily routine:

 6:45 a.m.	wake up	
 7:00 a.m.	eat a nut	
 7:15 a.m.	look at view	

12:00 noon

eat a nut

12:30 p.m.

look at view

5:00 p.m.

eat a nut

5:31 p.m.

look at view

8:00 p.m.

go to sleep

BUT let's say, just for example, that something unexpected **DID** happen ...

You can rest assured that this squirrel is prepared.

A few items in Scaredy Squirrel's emergency kit:

parachute

bug spray

mask and rubber gloves

hard hat	antibacterial soap	calamine lotion

net	Band-Aid	sardines

What to do in case of an emergency according to Scaredy Squirrel:

Dramatization

Step 1: Panic

Step 2: Run

Step 3: Get kit

Step 4: Put on kit

Step 5: Consult Exit Plan

Step 6: Exit tree (if there is absolutely, definitely, truly no other option)

Exit Plan *TOP SECRET*

Exit 1
Note to self:
Watch out for
green Martians
and killer bees
in the sky.

Exit 2
Note to self:
Do not land
in river. If
unavoidable,
use sardines
to distract
sharks.

I am here.

Exit 3
Note to self:
Look out for poison ivy
and for tarantulas roaming
the ground.

Exit 4
Note to self:
Keep in mind
that germs are
everywhere.

Remember, if all else fails, playing dead is always a good option!

With his emergency kit in hand, Scaredy Squirrel watches. Day after day he watches, until one day ...

A killer bee appears!

Scaredy Squirrel jumps in panic, knocking his emergency kit out of the tree.

This was **NOT** part of the Plan.

Scaredy Squirrel jumps to catch his kit.
He quickly regrets this idea.
The parachute is in the kit.

But something incredible happens . . .

Scaredy Squirrel is no ordinary squirrel.
He's a FLYING squirrel!

He starts to glide.

He feels overjoyed!

Adventurous!

Scaredy Squirrel forgets all about the killer bee, not to mention the tarantulas, poison ivy, green Martians, germs and sharks.

Finally Scaredy Squirrel realizes that nothing horrible is happening in the unknown today. So he returns to his nut tree.

All this excitement has inspired Scaredy Squirrel to make drastic changes to his life ...

Scaredy Squirrel's new-and-improved daily routine:

6:45 a.m.	wake up	
7:00 a.m.	eat a nut	
7:15 a.m.	look at view	
9:37 a.m.	jump into the unknown	

9:45 a.m.	play dead	
11:45 a.m.	return home	
12:00 noon	eat a nut	
12:30 p.m.	look at view	
5:00 p.m.	eat a nut	
5:31 p.m.	look at view	
8:00 p.m.	go to sleep	

poison ivy

P.S. As for the emergency kit, Scaredy Squirrel is in no hurry to pick it up just yet.

THE END

MÉLANIE WATT never leaves her home near Montreal, Quebec.

She would rather concentrate on creating books for kids.

Mélanie Watt's daily routine consists of waking up, eating, writing, drawing, erasing, drawing, eating and going to sleep.

Mélanie's books include:
LEON THE CHAMELEON
The LEARNING WITH ANIMALS collection
AUGUSTINE
SCAREDY SQUIRREL MAKES A FRIEND
CHESTER
SCAREDY SQUIRREL AT THE BEACH

P.S. Mélanie Watt is also afraid of sharks.